CIVIC PARTICIPATION
Working for Civil Rights

AMERICAN CIVIL RIGHTS MOVEMENT

Emily Mahoney

PowerKiDS
press™

New York

Published in 2017 by The Rosen Publishing Group, Inc.
29 East 21st Street, New York, NY 10010

First Edition

Editor: Caitlin McAneney
Book Design: Mickey Harmon

Photo Credits: Cover (image) -/Stringer/Getty Images; cover, pp. 1, 3–32 (background) Milena_Bo/ Shutterstock.com; p. 5 AFP/Stringer/AFP/Getty Images; p. 7 Hulton Archive/Staff/Hulton Archive/Getty Images; p. 9 (inset) https://commons.wikimedia.org/wiki/File:Harriet_Tubman_by_Squyer,_NPG,_c1885. jpg; p. 9 (main) UniversalImagesGroup/Contributor/Universal Images Group/Getty Images; p. 10 https:// commons.wikimedia.org/wiki/File:Abraham_Lincoln_O-55,_1861-crop.jpg; p. 11 https://commons. wikimedia.org/wiki/File:Union_soldiers_entrenched_along_the_west_bank_of_the_Rappahannock_River_at_ Fredericksburg,_Virginia_(111-B-157).jpg; p. 13 (main) Library of Congress/Contributor/Corbis Historical/ Getty Images; p. 13 (inset) https://commons.wikimedia.org/wiki/File:WEB_DuBois_1918.jpg; p. 14 https://commons.wikimedia.org/wiki/File:Malcolm_X_NYWTS_2a.jpg;
p. 15 https://commons.wikimedia.org/wiki/File:Martin_Luther_King,_Jr._and_Lyndon_Johnson_2.jpg;
p. 17 Bettmann/Contributor/Bettmann/Getty Images; p. 19 Thomas D. McAvoy/Contributor/The LIFE Picture Collection/Getty Images; p. 21 Francis Miller/Contributor/The LIFE Picture Collection/Getty Images; p. 23 (inset) Everett Historical/Shutterstock.com; p. 24 https://commons.wikimedia.org/wiki/ File:Lyndon_B._Johnson_Oval_Office_Portrait.tif; p. 25 Keystone/Stringer/Hulton Archive/Getty Images; p. 27 Bettmann/Contributor/Bettmann/Getty Images; p. 29 martinedoucet/Getty Images.

Library of Congress Cataloging-in-Publication Data

Names: Mahoney, Emily Jankowski, author.
Title: American civil rights movement / Emily Mahoney.
Description: New York : PowerKids Press, [2017] | Series: Civic participation
  : working for civil rights | Includes index.
Identifiers: LCCN 2016031522| ISBN 9781499427912 (pbk. book) | ISBN
  9781508152668 (6 pack) | ISBN 9781499428476 (library bound book)
Subjects: LCSH: African Americans–Civil rights–History–Juvenile
  literature. | Civil rights movements–United States–History–Juvenile
  literature. | United States–Race relations–Juvenile literature.
Classification: LCC E185.61 .M22 2017 | DDC 323.1196/073–dc23
LC record available at https://lccn.loc.gov/2016031522

Manufactured in the United States of America

CPSIA Compliance Information: Batch #BW17PK: For Further Information contact Rosen Publishing, New York, New York at 1-800-237-9932

CONTENTS

Fighting for Equal Rights 4

A History of Slavery 6

The Abolitionist Movement 8

A War Breaks Out 10

The NAACP Movement 12

Strong Leadership 14

The Montgomery Bus Boycott. 16

The Little Rock Nine 18

"I Have a Dream" 20

Violence Against African Americans. 22

The Civil Rights Act of 1964 24

The Voting Rights Act of 1965 26

The Fight's Not Over 28

Glossary. 31

Index 32

Websites 32

FIGHTING FOR EQUAL RIGHTS

Many people think of America as the land of freedom. However, for most of U.S. history, **minority** groups have been treated unfairly. African Americans were one of the first groups to band together to fight for equal rights. Their fight became known as the American civil rights movement. African Americans had to fight for many years for the right to vote and the right to use the same buildings and schools as white people.

Thanks to strong leaders, determined activists, and necessary **legislation**, African Americans now have the same legal rights as everyone else. However, we still have a long way to go in terms of social equality. This dangerous battle for equality is still being fought today.

The fight for civil rights has been long and difficult. Many people have given their lives for the cause. Today, people continue to fight for justice for all races.

A HISTORY OF SLAVERY

Slavery in North America started in 1619 when a slave ship brought enslaved Africans to the colony of Jamestown, which is in today's Virginia. These Africans may have been indentured servants, which meant they would earn their freedom and possibly money or land after a period of work. Over time, this system turned into true slavery. Slaves were considered to be a good thing in the colony because they were cheap and useful for farmwork.

Slavery continued after the founding of the United States. As tobacco and cotton plantations grew, more slaves were needed. Slaves were treated with violence and forced to work long hours. They were bought and sold as property, and families were often broken up.

In 1789, Olaudah Equiano wrote his life story, entitled *The Interesting Narrative of the Life of Olaudah Equiano, or Gustavus Vassa, the African*. He was taken from his home in Africa, sold into slavery, and eventually bought his freedom.

Rising Up

There were many reasons why most slaves didn't rise up against their owners. White landowners would punish or kill any slave who rebelled. Even so, some slaves tried to escape from their masters and some spoke out against slavery. A slave named Nat Turner led a slave revolt in Virginia in 1831. His group killed around 60 white people. Some African Americans, such as Frederick Douglass, learned to read and write in secret. Douglass used his abilities to write about the horrors and injustices of slavery.

THE ABOLITIONIST MOVEMENT

The movement to abolish, or end, slavery started growing in the 1830s. This was around the time of a religious movement called the Second Great Awakening. Followers of this movement wanted freedom for everyone. People who wanted an immediate end to slavery were known as radical abolitionists.

Most abolitionists took a peaceful approach to achieve their goals. An abolitionist named William Lloyd Garrison began to publish a newspaper called the *Liberator* in order to share his ideas. Others joined the American Anti-Slavery Society to show their support. This society formed in 1833 and was active until 1870. Branches of the society held public meetings with testimonies, or personal speeches, by former slaves. People who were against these antislavery activities often protested them violently. Angry mobs sometimes attacked speakers and disrupted meetings.

Many people tried to help slaves escape to freedom along a system of secret pathways and safe houses called the Underground Railroad. Harriet Tubman was an escaped slave who helped many other slaves make it to freedom on the Underground Railroad.

Harriet Tubman

A WAR BREAKS OUT

The American Civil War was fought between the Northern states, or the Union, and the Southern states, or the Confederacy. It started because of the many differences between the two regions, especially their views of slavery. The South had become dependent on slave labor, but all the Northern states had abolished slavery by 1804. The South seceded, or broke away, from the nation and declared itself a new nation. The war lasted from 1861 to 1865, and many people lost their lives during it.

Abraham Lincoln

Abraham Lincoln's election in 1860 was one of the reasons the Southern states left the nation. When he ran for president, Lincoln promised to keep slavery from spreading in the United States. He wanted to keep the country united, despite disagreements about slavery, and wouldn't recognize Southern states as a new nation. John Wilkes Booth, a man who agreed with the Confederacy, **assassinated** Lincoln on April 14, 1865.

After the American Civil War, important legislation was passed to give rights to African Americans. The 14th **Amendment** gave all former slaves citizenship. The 15th Amendment gave African American men the right to vote. Unfortunately, white people found ways to keep them from voting for another century.

In 1863, President Abraham Lincoln issued the Emancipation Proclamation, which freed all slaves in Confederate states that weren't under Union control. However, it wasn't until after the Confederacy surrendered in the spring of 1865 that slavery truly ended. That year, the 13th Amendment to the U.S. Constitution declared that slavery was illegal across the country.

THE NAACP MOVEMENT

The end of slavery didn't mean an end to **discrimination**. Southern states began creating policies and passing laws called black codes, which made it nearly impossible for African Americans to own land, get good jobs, or go to court against whites. Jim Crow laws made **segregation** legal. The 1896 Supreme Court case *Plessy v. Ferguson* said segregation was legal if facilities for blacks and whites were "separate but equal."

The NAACP, or the National Association for the Advancement of Colored People, was started in 1909 to deal with these issues. The NAACP Legal Defense and Education Fund was established in 1939 as the legal branch of the organization. It challenged unfair voting practices, segregation in universities, and segregation on buses traveling between states.

W. E. B. Du Bois, one of the
founders and leaders of the
NAACP, edited its magazine,
the *Crisis*, from 1910 to 1934.

STRONG LEADERSHIP

In order for change to occur, the American civil rights movement needed strong leadership. One of those strong leaders was Dr. Martin Luther King Jr., who was a key figure in the movement from the mid-1950s until his death in 1968. He was a clear choice as a leader because he was very smart and passionate about helping his fellow African Americans fight for equality.

Malcolm X

Malcolm X was another important leader in the fight for equality. He disagreed with Martin Luther King Jr.'s views on peaceful protest. He believed that more **aggressive** action was needed to gain equality, and he encouraged his followers to defend themselves, even if it meant being violent. While his views were more extreme than King's, they were both passionate about equality. Malcolm X was assassinated on February 21, 1965, at a rally for his organization.

Lyndon B. Johnson

Martin Luther King Jr.

On March 18, 1966, President Lyndon B. Johnson met with Martin Luther King Jr. at the White House.

King helped organize **boycotts**, protests, and legal actions. Many people respected him because he called for change through nonviolence. He was arrested many times, but this helped to raise awareness for his cause. Without King's hard work and determination, the movement may not have had the great success that it did. Unfortunately, King was assassinated on April 4, 1968, causing sadness throughout the country.

THE MONTGOMERY BUS BOYCOTT

The American civil rights movement was founded on the idea of using peace instead of violence to achieve equality. Members of the movement used boycotts and sit-ins to raise awareness for their cause.

An important boycott took place in Montgomery, Alabama, in 1955 and 1956. During this time, African American people were forced to give up their seats for white people on buses. A woman named Rosa Parks refused to do this and was arrested for breaking the law. Parks inspired other African Americans who followed her example.

Civil rights activists began refusing to take the bus system in Montgomery to show their anger with the unfair law. The transportation department lost money, and this boycott showed African Americans' outrage without resorting to violence.

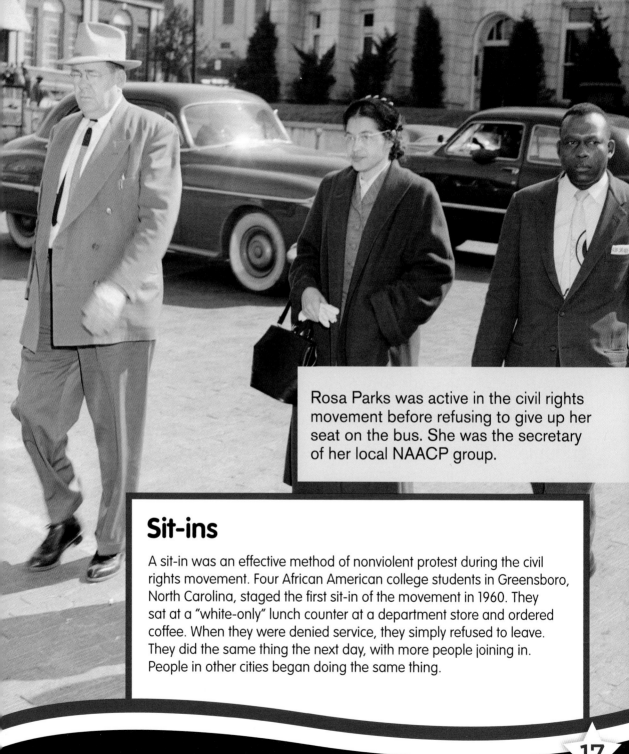

Rosa Parks was active in the civil rights movement before refusing to give up her seat on the bus. She was the secretary of her local NAACP group.

Sit-ins

A sit-in was an effective method of nonviolent protest during the civil rights movement. Four African American college students in Greensboro, North Carolina, staged the first sit-in of the movement in 1960. They sat at a "white-only" lunch counter at a department store and ordered coffee. When they were denied service, they simply refused to leave. They did the same thing the next day, with more people joining in. People in other cities began doing the same thing.

THE LITTLE ROCK NINE

Because of segregation, African Americans had to use public places that were **inferior** to those used by whites. It was important to integrate, or end segregation in, restaurants and movie theaters. However, it was most important to integrate schools so all children could receive the same education.

In September 1957, nine African American students showed up at Central High School in Little Rock, Arkansas, to start classes. The state National Guard stopped these students from entering the all-white school, but they didn't give up. Later in September, President Dwight D. Eisenhower called for troops to help escort the "Little Rock Nine" to their classes. It was an important step in ending the "separate but equal" rule in the United States.

Daisy Bates, president of the Arkansas branch of the NAACP, **recruited** the Little Rock Nine. Activists knew that many white people would protest integration, but they fought for the right to equal education anyway.

Brown v. Board of Education of Topeka

Brown v. Board of Education of Topeka was one of the most important Supreme Court cases during the civil rights movement. In 1954, the decision in this case said segregation of public schools was **unconstitutional**. This ruling also stated that "separate but equal" rules had no place in education. The Supreme Court noted that although schools were supposed to be "equal," many were not. This was the beginning of equality in education, but it would be years before schools were officially integrated.

"I HAVE A DREAM"

Perhaps the most well-known rally of the civil rights movement was the March on Washington. More than 200,000 people, black and white, gathered in Washington, D.C., on August 28, 1963. They were marching for equal access to jobs and equal rights. As this group of people walked through the streets of the nation's capital, they made speeches, sang songs, and said prayers. Martin Luther King Jr. gave his famous "I Have a Dream" speech. It encouraged people to work hard to change the unfair treatment that African Americans received.

The day ended with an important meeting between President John F. Kennedy and the leaders of the march to discuss changes. The Civil Rights Act of 1964 and the Voting Rights Act of 1965 reflected some of the requests and changes discussed that day.

The "I Have a Dream" speech is one of the most famous speeches in American history. In the speech, King said, "I have a dream that my four little children will one day live in a nation where they will not be judged by the color of their skin but by the content of their character."

VIOLENCE AGAINST AFRICAN AMERICANS

Before and during the civil rights movement, African Americans faced violence from white supremacists. White supremacists are people who believe that white people are superior to, or better than, people of other races. They believe that white people should have control over people of other races.

The Ku Klux Klan (KKK) was established in 1865 in Tennessee. KKK members held violent riots that targeted African Americans, especially those who were fighting for equality. Members of the KKK wore white hooded robes. They burned buildings and killed many black people and activists. The group disbanded, but members became active again in the South during the civil rights movement. On September 15, 1963, the KKK bombed the 16th Street Baptist Church in Birmingham, Alabama. Unfortunately, the KKK still exists today.

Ku Klux Klan

The bombing of the 16th Street Baptist Church killed four young girls. This church had been a center for the African American community in Birmingham.

THE CIVIL RIGHTS ACT OF 1964

In 1964, the civil rights movement celebrated a huge victory for justice. President Lyndon B. Johnson signed the Civil Rights Act of 1964 into law. This act officially ended segregation in public places. It also banned job discrimination on the basis of race, color, religion, sex, or national origin. This was such an important step for the movement because it finally ended the "separate but equal" laws that dated back to the 1800s.

Because of the Civil Rights Act of 1964, African Americans could no longer legally be denied service at businesses because of the color of their skin. Places such as parks, theaters, restaurants, and hotels couldn't be segregated anymore. This law is still in effect today, and it has been expanded to include other minority groups.

Lyndon B. Johnson

In his first State of the Union address, Johnson said, "Let this session of Congress be known as the session which did more for civil rights than the last hundred sessions combined."

THE VOTING RIGHTS ACT OF 1965

Another great victory for African Americans came in 1965 when the Voting Rights Act was passed. This allowed African Americans to finally have a voice in the government. President Johnson signed this bill into law on August 6, 1965. It was designed to protect African Americans' right to vote despite state and local laws that made it difficult. Poll taxes and literacy, or reading, tests kept many African Americans from voting even though they were supposed to have that right.

The Voting Rights Act was passed partly in response to a voting rights march that started from Selma, Alabama, on March 7, 1965. The peaceful march soon turned violent when Alabama state troopers attacked the marchers. Some marchers were beaten and many were injured.

African American women wait in line to vote in 1965 at the Alabama Dallas County Courthouse.

THE FIGHT'S NOT OVER

The United States has come a long way from the days of slavery, black codes, and segregation. Thanks to strong leaders and activists in the civil rights movement, African Americans now have equality under the law. **Initiatives** are in place to improve educational and employment opportunities for people of minority groups.

However, racism still exists in the United States. Minorities are underrepresented in branches of government. More African Americans are in jail or prison than whites, and they often receive longer prison sentences. The fight for social equality is far from over.

What can you do to help? Treat others with respect and fairness, regardless of their race. Educate others about the American civil rights movement and celebrate the work and **legacy** of the leaders who gave their lives for equality.

The first step towards ending discrimination of any kind is to be tolerant, or accepting, of people who are different from you.

TIMELINE OF THE CIVIL RIGHTS MOVEMENT

1787
The Three-Fifths Compromise is reached during the U.S. Constitutional Convention. Under it, slaves count as three-fifths of a white person when calculating a state's representation in government.

1831
Nat Turner leads a slave revolt in Virginia.

1861
The Civil War begins.

1865
The Civil War ends.

1870s
The first Jim Crow laws are passed. These laws enforced segregation in southern states.

1909
The NAACP is formed.

1954
In *Brown vs. Board of Education*, the Supreme Court rules that segregation of public schools is illegal.

1955
Rosa Parks refuses to give up her seat for a white bus passenger.

1956
The Montgomery bus boycott ends in victory for the civil rights movement.

1963
Martin Luther King Jr. delivers his "I Have a Dream" speech at the March on Washington.

1964
The Civil Rights Act is passed.

1965
The Voting Rights Act is passed.

GLOSSARY

aggressive: Acting with forceful energy and determination.

amendment: A change or addition to a constitution.

assassinate: To kill someone, usually for political reasons.

boycott: To join with others in refusing to buy from or deal with a person, nation, or business.

discrimination: The practice of treating a person or group differently because of their race or beliefs.

inferior: Less than or worse than something else.

initiative: A program or plan that's intended to solve a problem.

legacy: The lasting effect of a person or thing.

legislation: Laws.

minority: A group of people who are different from a larger population in some way.

recruit: To seek out suitable people and get them to join an organization or cause.

segregation: The forced separation of people based on race, class, or ethnicity.

unconstitutional: Going against the constitution of a country or government.

INDEX

A
abolitionists, 8
American Anti-Slavery
    Society, 8

B
Bates, Daisy, 19
black codes, 12, 28
Booth, John Wilkes, 10
*Brown v. Board of
    Education of Topeka,*
    19, 30

C
Civil Rights Act of 1964,
    20, 24, 30
Civil War, American, 10,
    11, 30
Confederacy, 10, 11
Crisis, 13

D
Douglass, Frederick, 7
Du Bois, W. E. B., 13

E
Eisenhower, Dwight D., 18
Emancipation
    Proclamation, 11
Equiano, Olaudah, 7

G
Garrison, William Lloyd, 8

J
Jamestown, 6
Jim Crow laws, 12, 30
Johnson, Lyndon B., 15,
    24, 25, 26

K
Kennedy, John F., 20
King, Martin Luther, Jr., 14,
    15, 20, 21, 30
Ku Klux Klan, 22, 23

L
Liberator, 8
Lincoln, Abraham, 10, 11
Little Rock Nine, 18, 19

M
Malcolm X, 14
March on Washington,
    20, 30
Montgomery bus boycott,
    16, 30

N
NAACP, 12, 13, 17,
    19, 30

P
Parks, Rosa, 16, 17
Plessy v. Ferguson, 12

S
Second Great
    Awakening, 8
segregation, 12, 18, 19,
    24, 28, 30
sit-ins, 16, 17
16th Street Baptist
    Church, 22, 23
Supreme Court, 12,
    19, 30

T
Tubman, Harriet, 9
Turner, Nat, 7, 30

U
Underground Railroad, 9

V
Voting Rights Act of 1965,
    20, 30

W
white supremacists, 22

WEBSITES

Due to the changing nature of Internet links, PowerKids Press has developed an online
list of websites related to the subject of this book. This site is updated regularly. Please
use this link to access the list: www.powerkidslinks.com/civic/civil